I0766480

Dedication of the book:

To Ken, my rock, and biggest supporter. Thank you for cheering me on. To Daire, thank you for all the input and encouragement you have given me. And to Lorcan, thank you for being the inspiration to write this and for your input, support, and motivation. I love you all.

About the author:

Erin Finnigan is a mother who enjoys travel, baking, and reading. She lives in Massachusetts with her husband, Ken, and two sons. Monster Wand is her first story.

Description of the book:

Lorcan has no fear during his daytime adventures fighting monsters. Night time is another story. With the help from Papa, Lorcan learns how to be brave.

Acknowledgements

A heartfelt thank you to all the wonderful people who made this book possible. To my family, for their endless support and encouragement, and for inspiring my imagination with stories of their own. To my amazing illustrator Brian, whose vibrant artwork brought my characters to life in ways I could only dream of.

I d also like to thank the teachers and librarians who inspire young readers every day and remind us all of the magic of stories. A special shoutout to my children who shared their thoughts and ideas during the writing process you are the true inspiration behind this adventure!

Finally, to all the little dreamers out there, may this book spark your imagination and remind you that anything is possible. Happy reading!

This is Lorcan.
Lorcan loves to use his imagination.

Every day he sets off on new adventures to far off places.

Daytime monsters are no match for the brave Lorcan.

Nighttime monsters, however, are different.

"There are no such things as monsters," Lorcan's mom tells him as she tucks him back into bed.

Lorcan doesn't believe her.

Every day Lorcan fights off the monsters in his adventures,

but at night he still can't sleep.

"I've got just the thing to make the monsters go away."
says Papa, "It is a magical monster wand."

"Papa that is a wooden spoon!"
Lorcan says looking confused.

YEL

RED
GLUE
"It might look like a spoon,
but once we decorate it,
it becomes a monster wand.
We can decorate it together."

"Let's give it a try!"
Papa exclaims,
"Repeat after me
'monsters be gone!'
as you wave your wand."
RED

Lorcan repeats what Papa says.

Every night before bed Lorcan waves
his monster wand and calls out...

"MONSTERS BE GONE!"

It works.
The monsters are gone.

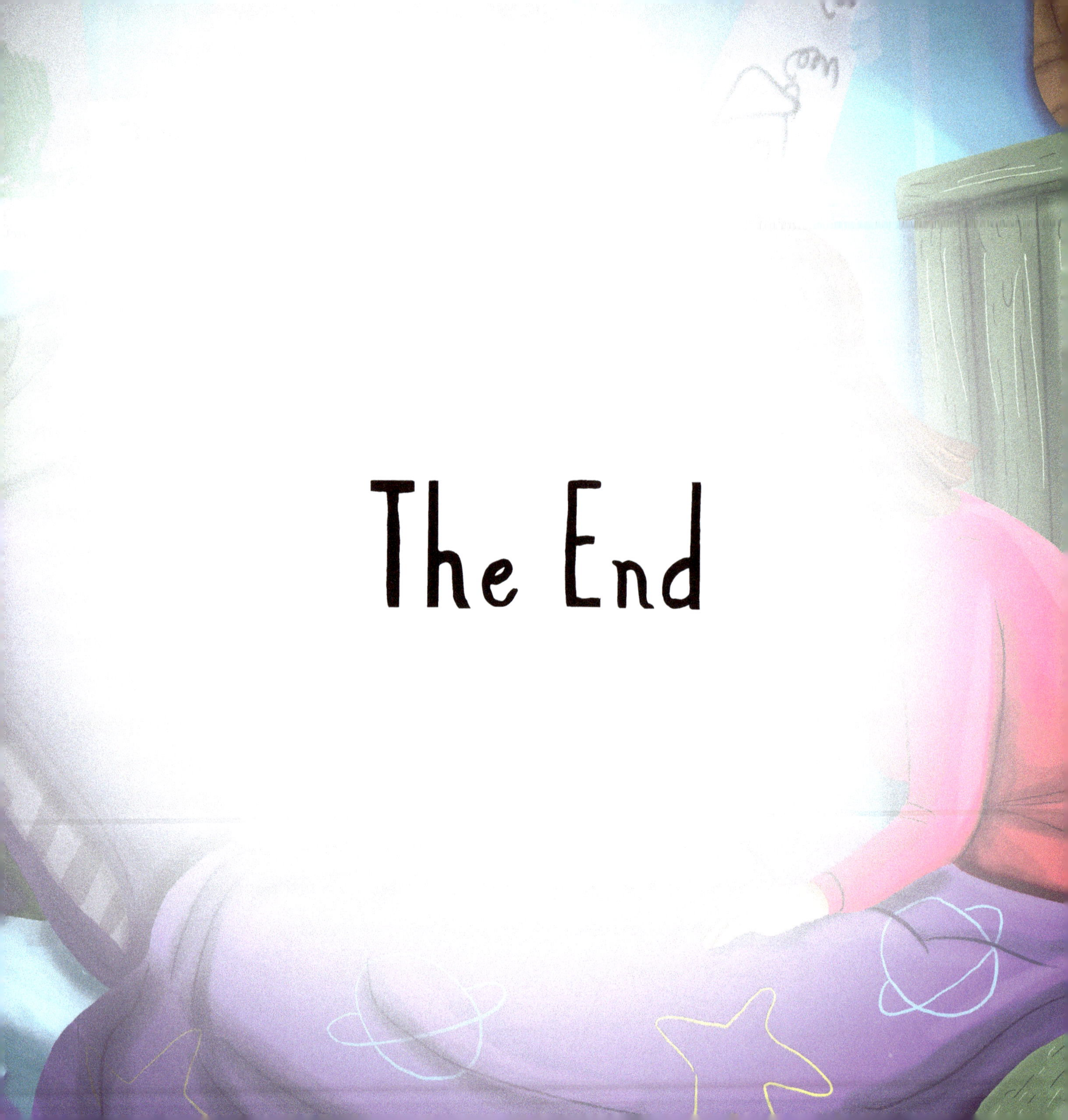
The End

www.ingramcontent.com/pod-product-compliance
Lightning Source LLC
Chambersburg PA
CBHW041156300726
48981CB00004B/271